D0617458

ORCHARD BOOKS
338 Euston Road, London NW1 3BH
*Orchard Books Australia*
Level 17/207 Kent Street, Sydney, NSW 2000
A Paperback Original

First published in 2009 by Orchard Books.

© 2009 Rainbow Magic Limited.
A HIT Entertainment company. Rainbow Magic is a trademark of Rainbow Magic Limited. Reg. U.S. Pat. & Tm. Off. And other countries.

Illustrations © Orchard Books 2009

A CIP catalogue record for this book is available from the British Library.

ISBN 978 1 40830 354 2
1 3 5 7 9 10 8 6 4 2

Printed in China by Imago

Orchard Books is a division of Hachette Children's Books, an Hachette UK company

www.hachette.co.uk

# Leona the Unicorn Fairy

by Daisy Meadows

ORCHARD BOOKS

www.rainbowmagic.co.uk

The Fairyland Palace
Barn
Farmhouse
Stables
Clubhouse
CAMP
Adventure Lake
Birdwatching Tower

Jack Frost's
Ice Castle
Meadows
Amphitheatre
The Labyrinth
Maze of tunnels
Cabins
Waterfall
Hills

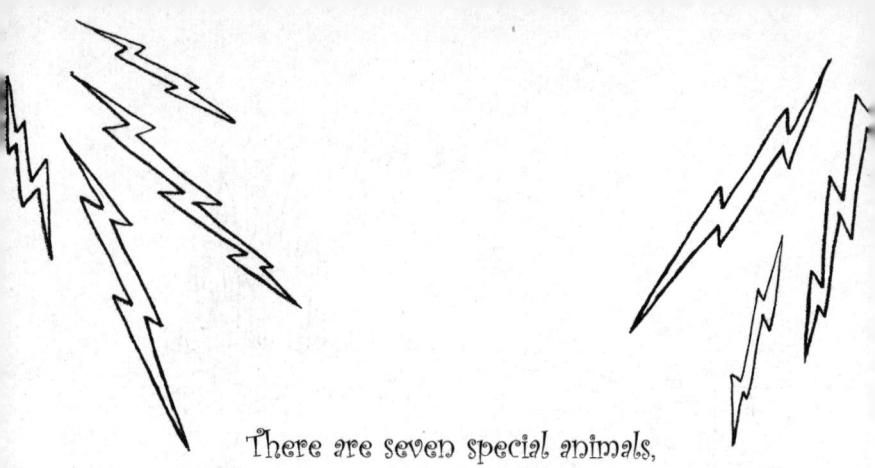

There are seven special animals,
Who live in Fairyland.
They use their magic powers
To help others where they can.

A dragon, black cat, firebird,
A seahorse and snow swan too,
A unicorn and ice bear -
I know just what to do.

I'll lock them in my castle
And never let them out.
The world will turn more miserable,
Of that, I have no doubt...

# Contents


| | |
|---|---|
| Spooked! | 9 |
| The Unicorn Appears | 21 |
| Leona's Lollipop | 31 |
| Twisty on the Loose | 45 |
| A Ransom Note | 59 |
| Ponies to the Rescue | 67 |

# Spooked!

"Isn't this great, Kirsty?" Rachel Walker twisted round in her saddle to smile at her best friend, Kirsty Tate. "I'd only ever been horseriding once or twice before, but now I just love it!" And Rachel patted her chestnut pony, Sparkle.

"Me too," agreed Kirsty, who was on a beautiful black pony behind Rachel.

The girls had been having riding lessons ever since they arrived at camp, but this was the first time they'd been on a trail ride through the forest. "I think it's because Sparkle and Tansy are so sweet. They don't mind if we do something wrong!"

"Keep following the trail, everyone," called Susan, their riding instructor, from the back of the line. There were several other campers on ponies in front of and behind Kirsty and Rachel. "It will lead us back to the camp eventually."

"I can't believe we've only got a day and a half left at camp," Rachel sighed as the ponies ambled on through the forest. It was cool and shady under the trees, but beams of sunlight dappled the grass here and there. "We've had *such* a good time, haven't we, Kirsty? We've tried hiking, orienteering, bird-watching and caving, and we've made some great friends."

But Kirsty wasn't really listening. She was staring around, peering through the trees on either side of the trail.

"Sorry, Rachel," she said quickly. "I was just seeing if I could spot anything unusual..."

Rachel smiled. She knew exactly what Kirsty was looking for! On the day the girls arrived at camp, the King and Queen of Fairyland had asked for their help.

Kirsty and Rachel had discovered that Jack Frost and his goblin servants had kidnapped seven magical young animals from the Magical Animal Fairies. These animals had the power to spread the kind of magical qualities that every human and fairy could possess – the magic of imagination, luck, humour, friendship, compassion, healing and courage. It was the fairies' job to train the Magical Animals for a whole year to make sure they knew how to use their magic properly. Then the animals would use their incredible powers to bring happiness to both the human and the fairy worlds.

But Jack Frost was determined to disrupt the Magical Animals' training because he didn't want *anyone*, humans or fairies, to be happy. So, with the help of his goblins, Jack Frost had stolen the animals from Fairyland and imprisoned them in his Ice Castle. But the young animals had managed to escape and had hidden themselves away in the human world. Jack Frost had sent his goblins to find them, but the Magical Animal Fairies had asked Rachel and Kirsty to help them track down the animals and return them safely to Fairyland.

"Remember what Queen Titania says, Kirsty," Rachel whispered. "It doesn't always help to look for magic. You must let the magic find *you!*"

"I know," Kirsty replied, "But it's *so* difficult! I just want to find Leona's unicorn and Caitlin's ice bear. I'm worried about them because they haven't learned how to use their magical powers properly yet."

"We're doing OK, though," Rachel pointed out. "We've already found Ashley's dragon, Lara's little black cat, Erin's firebird, Rihanna's seahorse and Sophia's snow swan."

"That's true," Kirsty said with a smile. "Let's just enjoy the trail ride and wait for the magic to come to us!"

Rachel nodded. "Look, Kirsty, there's another fox," she said, catching a glimpse of russet brown between the trees. "That makes two we've seen now."

"Yes, as well as three rabbits and six squirrels!" Kirsty replied. "There's lots of wildlife around here, isn't there?"

Suddenly, without any warning at all, the pony in front of Rachel and Kirsty gave a frightened little neigh and reared upwards. Lauren, the camper riding the pony, gasped with fright.

"Quick, Rachel!" Kirsty cried urgently, spotting a side path to her left. "Down here!"

Swiftly Kirsty and Rachel pulled Tansy and Sparkle off the trail and down the side path to avoid a collision.

Meanwhile Lauren got her pony, Sky, under control again.

"Are you all right, girls?" called Susan, trotting towards them. "Looks like Sky got spooked by something."

"I'm fine," said Lauren, patting Sky's neck. Rachel and Kirsty nodded in agreement.

"Good thinking, you two," Susan went on, smiling at them. "You got your ponies out of the way just in time."

As the riders moved on again, Kirsty and Rachel turned their ponies around to rejoin the main path. But then, Kirsty saw a sudden flash of bright green in the undergrowth around her. Immediately she turned to her friend.

"Rachel!" Kirsty gasped. "I just saw something green – and it definitely wasn't anything leafy!"

"Do you think it was a goblin?" Rachel whispered, alarmed. "Maybe there's more wildlife in this forest than we thought!"

"It *could* have been a goblin that scared Lauren's pony," Kirsty suggested.

"We'll check it out," Rachel said. "Let's hang back and join the end of the line."

The girls waited until the other campers had ridden past, and then they trotted back onto the trail some distance behind them. They kept a sharp look-out for goblins, but didn't see anything.

Then Rachel heard a rustling in the bushes. Before she could say anything to Kirsty, two goblins jumped out onto the path, right in front of them!

# The Unicorn Appears

"Oh!" Kirsty gasped, quickly bringing Tansy to a halt. Rachel did the same with Sparkle.

The biggest goblin nudged the smaller one and pointed at the two ponies.

"Is one of those a unicorn?" he whispered in a loud voice.

Rachel glanced at Kirsty. These goblins must be looking for Leona's unicorn, one of the missing Magical Animals!

The smallest goblin looked disgusted. "Are you stupid?" he demanded. "These are ponies, not unicorns! Unicorns have a horn on top of their heads—"

"Don't call me stupid!" the other goblin screeched furiously.

"Well, you *are* stupid!" the smallest goblin yelled. "Whoever heard of a unicorn without a horn?"

Arguing loudly, the two goblins began shoving each other.

Kirsty was alarmed. The path was too narrow for them to get past the fighting goblins, and they were coming closer to the girls' ponies.

"Look out!" Kirsty called.

The biggest goblin pushed the smaller one in front of Rachel's pony. Sparkle gave a loud, startled neigh and reared up. The goblins yelped in alarm and shot off through the undergrowth.

"It's OK, Sparkle!" Rachel gasped, trying to get the frightened pony under control. But Sparkle bolted off at top speed through the trees, with Rachel clinging desperately to the reins.

"Oh no!" Kirsty cried, horrified. "Hold on, Rachel!" And she urged Tansy after them.

Rachel's heart was pounding anxiously as Sparkle galloped through the forest. She had to keep ducking to avoid low branches, and she was very worried that either she'd fall off the pony or that a branch would hit her.

"Whoa, Sparkle!" she called. Remembering what they'd been taught in their riding lessons, Rachel squeezed Sparkle's flanks with her legs and pulled back on the reins. But unfortunately Sparkle slowed down and stopped too quickly. Rachel wasn't expecting this, and she flew right over the pony's head.

"Rachel!" Kirsty shouted, cantering up behind Sparkle just in time to see her friend go sailing through the air.

To Kirsty's relief, she saw that Rachel had landed on a soft, springy patch of moss on the forest floor. Jumping quickly down from Tansy, Kirsty rushed over to her friend.

"Are you OK, Rachel?" Kirsty asked, kneeling down beside her. She could see that Rachel was holding her arm, looking rather shaken.

"I'm fine, except I think I've sprained my wrist," Rachel replied, wincing. "It hurts a lot."

"I'll run after Susan and get help," Kirsty said, glancing round. "They can't have got much further up the trail."

But at that moment, a gleam of pure, dazzling white among the trees caught Kirsty's eye. It appeared to be coming straight towards them.

"Rachel, look!" Kirsty gasped in wonder as the white shape came closer. "It's a *unicorn*."

"It's Leona's missing Magical Animal!" Rachel whispered, her eyes wide.

The beautiful young unicorn came trotting through the trees towards them. He was about the size of a Shetland pony, and his coat was gleaming white. He had shining golden hooves and a twisted golden horn on his head.

The unicorn stopped a few metres from Rachel and Kirsty. He lowered his snow-white head, shaking his long mane, and suddenly a shower of golden glitter burst from his horn. It flew through the air and encircled Rachel's injured wrist like a dazzling bracelet.

The girls could hardly believe their eyes. A few seconds later, the glitter began to dissolve in a sparkling mist.

"Rachel! Kirsty! Where are you?"

"That's Susan," Kirsty said as they heard the sound of a horse's hooves. "She's looking for us."

The unicorn's ears pricked up. Quickly he turned and galloped off through the trees.

"Oh, please come back!" Rachel called after him. She turned to Kirsty, looking worried. "However will we find him again, Kirsty?

"I don't know." Kirsty frowned. "Let's just hope the goblins don't find him first!"

Kirsty put out her hand to help Rachel to her feet. As she stood up, Rachel suddenly gave a gasp.

"Is your wrist hurting?" Kirsty asked sympathetically.

Rachel shook her head. "No, that's just it," she replied, bending her wrist this way and that. "It's all better!"

"I've just remembered," Kirsty said excitedly. "The unicorn's magical power is healing. He must have healed your wrist with the glitter from his horn!"

At that moment Susan rode through the trees towards them.

"Are you OK, girls?" she asked, dismounting quickly and coming over to them. "We suddenly realised that you weren't with us on the trail."

"Sparkle got spooked and bolted," Rachel explained. She hoped the goblins weren't anywhere around. It would be a disaster if Susan spotted them because no one was meant to know that Fairyland existed. "But I'm fine."

"Lucky you were wearing your riding-hat, or your injuries could have been a lot worse," Susan said, as she checked Rachel over.

Rachel winked at Kirsty. "Luck and the healing touch of a unicorn!" she whispered, as Susan went to check Sparkle for injuries, too.

"Right, time to get back to camp," Susan said briskly. "I think you've had enough excitement for one day, and your free-time session is coming up, so you won't want to miss that."

Reluctantly, Rachel and Kirsty climbed back onto their ponies.

"I don't want to leave the unicorn in the forest all alone," Kirsty said anxiously to Rachel as they followed Susan back to the trail. "Not with the goblins around!"

"Let's come back and search for the unicorn when we've put Sparkle and Tansy in the stables," Rachel suggested.

Back at the camp Rachel and Kirsty led their ponies into their shared stall and carefully began to brush them down. The stable door was open and, as Rachel and Kirsty brushed their ponies' manes, they heard voices outside.

"Do you know if any ponies have escaped from the stables, Katie?" someone asked. Kirsty and Rachel recognised the voice. It was Emma, one of their dorm-mates. "I think I saw a small white pony heading towards the amphitheatre just now."

"Really? You must be seeing things!" Katie said teasingly. "There aren't any white ponies here."

Kirsty and Rachel glanced at each other in alarm. The amphitheatre was a round, open-air theatre where the campers could put on shows and perform plays.

So the unicorn had come to the camp!

"That's what I thought." Emma sounded very puzzled. "What's *really* weird though is that it looked like the pony had a twisted horn on its head!"

"Maybe it's a unicorn?" Katie suggested, laughing.

Emma laughed too. "It's probably just a practical joke," she said. "The campers and counsellors have been playing funny tricks on each other all week, haven't they? I found a plastic frog inside one of my wellies this morning!"

Rachel turned to Kirsty as the other two girls walked away, still laughing.

"I think the unicorn must have followed us back to camp!" Rachel exclaimed. "We *have* to find him before someone realises he's a *real* unicorn."

"Or he's captured by the goblins," Kirsty added.

Quickly, Rachel and Kirsty gave Tansy and Sparkle their buckets of oats, as well as a few carrots for a treat. Then they rushed out of the stall.

"Rachel?" Susan popped out of one of the other stalls as they went by. "I want you to stop by the first-aid cabin and see Elizabeth, the camp nurse."

"But I'm fine," Rachel insisted.

"It can't do any harm to be sure, can it?" Susan said kindly. "Off you go."

Rachel's face fell as Susan went back into the stall.

"I hope this doesn't take too long," she said anxiously as she and Kirsty hurried off to the first-aid cabin.

"Ah, there you are, Rachel." Elizabeth was at her desk rolling up bandages when the girls knocked and went in. She was young and friendly with a snow-white uniform and long red hair pinned neatly back. "Let's take a look at you. Any bumps or bruises?"

Rachel shook her head.

"Well, you seem fine," Elizabeth remarked a few minutes later with a smile. "I think you can safely go off and enjoy the rest of the afternoon."

"Thanks, Elizabeth," Rachel said, jumping eagerly to her feet. "Sorry to have wasted your time."

"Oh, it was nice to have something to do," Elizabeth replied. "I usually see a dozen or more campers every day with various scrapes and bruises, but you're the only ones I've seen so far today." She picked up another roll of bandages. "So I decided to tidy my medicine cupboard instead."

"That's because of Leona's unicorn," Kirsty whispered to Rachel as they went to the door of the cabin. "His healing powers mean the campers don't need the nurse!"

"Help yourself to a lollipop from my jar on your way out, girls," Elizabeth called.

There was a big glass jar of brightly coloured lollipops on a shelf near the door. As Rachel lifted it down, she noticed that the jar was glowing strangely.

"What's going on?" Rachel whispered to Kirsty, her eyes wide with amazement as she unscrewed the lid.

Kirsty looked excited. She put her hand into the jar and pulled out a red strawberry-flavoured lollipop. Clinging to the top of it was a tiny fairy!

Kirsty just about managed not to cry out in surprise. She and Rachel smiled down at the fairy, who wore wide-legged blue trousers, a matching shrug and a starry gold belt. Her long blonde hair was tied up in a ponytail.

"Hello, girls!" the fairy called in a low voice, her eyes twinkling. "I'm so glad I've found you! Remember me? I'm Leona the Unicorn Fairy."

"Hello, Leona," Rachel and Kirsty whispered back.

Quickly the girls went out of the first-aid cabin, Kirsty carrying the lollipop.

"As you know, I'm looking for my unicorn, Twisty," Leona explained. "I thought he might be attracted to the first-aid cabin because he has special healing powers." She looked anxiously at Rachel and Kirsty. "Have you seen him?"

"Yes, but not here," Rachel told Leona.

And quickly she explained how Twisty had appeared in the forest and healed her injured wrist.

"But now we think Twisty is right here in the camp!" Kirsty added. "Emma, our dorm-mate, saw him near the amphitheatre. But don't worry, Leona, she thought it was some sort of joke."

Leona looked relieved. "We'd better get to the amphitheatre right away!" she said. She dived into Kirsty's pocket out of sight, and the girls hurried off.

The amphitheatre was at the edge of the camp. As they approached it, Rachel blinked several times in surprise. She could see human-sized fairies dancing around the stage wearing floaty white dresses and with gauzy wings on their shoulders.

"They're not *real* fairies, Rachel," Kirsty said with a grin. "They're just campers in costume! Look, one of them is Catherine from our dorm."

"You're right," Rachel agreed. "For a minute there I thought we had some visitors from Fairyland!"

A Fairy King and Queen, wearing golden crowns, were also dancing amongst the fairies. As the girls got closer to the stage, Kirsty did a double take. Was that a *goblin* skipping along next to the Fairy Queen? But when Kirsty looked again, there was no one there.

"I've got goblins on the brain!" Kirsty thought, shaking her head.

"Katrina," Rachel called to a camper who was watching the dancers. "What's going on?"

"Oh, this is a rehearsal for Shakespeare's play, *A Midsummer Night's Dream*," Katrina explained.

At that moment another camper called Tom wandered past. He heard what Katrina was saying and looked confused.

"Hey, Katrina, there isn't a *unicorn* in the play, is there?" he asked.

Rachel and Kirsty exchanged glances as Katrina shook her head.

"No, why?"

Tom laughed. "Someone must have attached a horn to a Shetland pony's head for a joke then!" he replied. "I just saw it leave the amphitheatre and trot towards the clubhouse."

"Well, there aren't supposed to be any goblins in this play either." Katrina shrugged. "But I've seen two campers dressed up as goblins this afternoon!"

Rachel and Kirsty both gasped with horror. So the goblins were at the camp too!

"I even overheard one of the actors refuse to take off his goblin costume," Katrina said with a laugh. "Some people really get into their parts!"

"We'd better go straight to the clubhouse," Leona whispered, popping her head out of Kirsty's pocket as the girls hurried off. "The goblins are on Twisty's trail too. We *must* find him before they do!"

Rachel and Kirsty ran to the clubhouse. They had a quick look around outside, but couldn't see Twisty.

"What are we going to do, Rachel?" Kirsty asked desperately. "We can't run around the camp all day!"

"Let's ask inside if anyone's seen anything," Rachel suggested.

The girls rushed into the clubhouse. Some of the campers were playing ping pong and pool while others watched a movie on TV.

Rachel went over to the boys playing pool. "Sorry to bother you," she said, "but have you seen a pony dressed up to look like a unicorn today?"

"I did," said one of the boys. "When I was playing football."

"What happened?" Rachel asked eagerly.

"Well, I fell over and skinned my knees," the boy explained. "I had to come off the pitch and that pony was standing there watching me. Then it shook its mane and showered glitter over me!" The boy laughed. "I guess someone was trying to trick me into thinking it was a magic unicorn!"

Kirsty and Rachel glanced down at the boy's knees. They didn't look badly grazed at all.

"Maybe the unicorn helped heal the boy, just like he did for you, Rachel," Kirsty whispered.

"I saw the pretend unicorn down by the dock at the lake," another boy at the pool table added. "It looks really realistic! I tried to get a closer look, but he trotted off."

Rachel and Kirsty hurried out of the clubhouse.

"So Twisty could be in *two* places," Rachel said as Leona popped out of Kirsty's pocket. "The sports pitch or the lake."

"If we choose the wrong one, we might miss him," Leona pointed out anxiously.

"Maybe we should split up," suggested Kirsty. "Leona could go to the lake because it's further away and flying will be quicker. Rachel and I can search the sports pitch."

Leona nodded. "Good thinking, Kirsty," she said. "I'll meet you back at the stables in fifteen minutes."

And Leona rose up into the air and zoomed away, her blonde hair flying.

"I don't like being away from Leona, but we *have* to find Twisty before someone realises he's a real unicorn," Rachel sighed, as she and Kirsty dashed off.

"Or before the goblins find him!" Kirsty added.

The girls raced to the sports pitch and began to search around. But to their disappointment, Twisty wasn't there.

"What now?" Rachel asked.

"I suppose we'd better head back to the stables to meet Leona," Kirsty began. But then she broke off as a flash of white in the forest that bordered the sports pitch caught her eye.

"Rachel!" Kirsty cried. "It's Twisty!"

# A Ransom Note

"Careful!" Rachel whispered. She gazed at the unicorn who was grazing on the grass between the trees. "We mustn't frighten him."

The girls sneaked across the pitch and up to the unicorn. As they tiptoed towards him, Rachel wondered how they could catch him and take him back to Leona. Then suddenly she realised she still had a carrot in her pocket from feeding their ponies earlier. She took it out and showed it silently to Kirsty, who nodded.

"Here, Twisty," Rachel called, holding the carrot a little way from the unicorn's nose.

Twisty raised his head and sniffed the carrot. Rachel moved away a little and the unicorn walked after her, his beautiful dark eyes fixed on the carrot just in front of him.

Rachel led Twisty through the forest,

then took a back route towards the stables so that they would be less likely to bump into other campers. Kirsty went in front, keeping a sharp look-out to make sure no one else was about.

When they reached the stables, both girls sighed with relief. They patted Twisty, who shook his mane and gave a little neigh.

"Thank you for healing my wrist today, Twisty," Rachel said, feeding the carrot to the unicorn.

"I wonder where Leona is?" Kirsty said with a frown, glancing around as Twisty crunched up his carrot. Suddenly she spotted a piece of paper stuck to the door of the stables. "What's that, Rachel?"

"It looks like a note," Rachel replied. "What does it say?"

The note was in shaky handwriting in green ink. It read:

We have the fairi
We want the unikorn
we will trade u
meet us behind the stables
Now!!! The Goblins

"I don't believe it!" Rachel cried. "The goblins aren't smart enough to catch Leona."

"Or *any* fairy!" Kirsty agreed. "It might be a trap. But we'd better go and meet them, just in case."

Quickly the girls led Twisty around the back of the stables. They held on tightly to the unicorn, afraid that the goblins might pounce and try to steal him.

The two goblins who'd spooked Sparkle in the forest earlier were standing by the ponies' trough. The smallest one was holding Nurse Elizabeth's lollipop jar. As Rachel, Kirsty and Twisty came closer, the goblin shook the jar. It sparkled in the sun like magic fairy dust.

"Oh no!" Rachel whispered to Kirsty. "Maybe the goblins *have* captured Leona in that big jar!"

But Kirsty shook her head. "No, Leona would use her magic to escape, wouldn't she?" she replied. "It could just be something else sparkling inside the jar."

The goblin holding the lollipop jar turned his back towards Rachel and Kirsty.

"I'm trapped, girls!" he called in a high-pitched, squeaky voice. "Help me! I mean, *please* in a sparkly, fairy way!"

Rachel and Kirsty tried not to laugh. It was really obvious that the goblin was only pretending to have Leona!

"Hand over that unicorn!" the other goblin demanded, stepping forward, "and we'll let your fairy friend go."

At that moment Rachel and Kirsty noticed a twinkling light whizzing through the air towards the goblins. It was Leona! Now the girls *knew* the goblins were bluffing.

"We know you don't have Leona," Rachel said firmly.

"We *do* have her!" The goblin stamped his foot in a rage. "We captured her when she was flying towards the lake."

"And we know she's not with you," the goblin with the jar said triumphantly, "Or the unicorn wouldn't still be here!"

"But *we* know where Leona is," Kirsty said, and she and Rachel both pointed above the goblins' heads.

"Don't try to trick us!" the goblin with the jar jeered. "We've been fooled by you before. Now, give us the unicorn!"

# Ponies to the Rescue

Suddenly Leona swooped down, waving cheekily at the goblins. They shrieked with surprise.

"Get her!" the biggest goblin roared.

Quickly, the other goblin unscrewed the jar. He pulled out a handful of glitter and tossed it at Leona. The fairy was forced to dart and dodge around to avoid the sparkles.

"We have to help Leona!" Kirsty gasped. "Keep hold of Twisty, Rachel!"

Rachel nodded. Immediately Kirsty dashed forward. She had to distract the goblins *somehow.* As the goblin threw another shower of sparkles at Leona, Kirsty rushed over to Tansy's and Sparkle's stall.

"Tansy, Sparkle!" she called.

When the ponies saw Kirsty, they immediately stuck their heads out of the open top of the door to be stroked. They neighed happily and the goblins almost jumped out of their skins.

"Help!" shouted the biggest goblin in terror. "It's those scary ponies again!"

The smallest goblin also gave a yell of surprise. He dropped the lollipop jar, spilling glitter on the ground. Kirsty snatched the jar up.

But as Leona headed towards Twisty, the biggest goblin made one last attempt to catch her. He gave a giant leap, but Leona slipped neatly through his fingers. The goblin sailed through the air and landed with a thud in a pile of horse manure.

"Yuk, gross!" sniggered the smallest goblin.

"Here, Twisty!" Leona called, holding out her arms as she flew towards the unicorn.

Smiling, Rachel released Twisty. He cantered upwards and bounded through the air to Leona. As he did so, he shrank down to his tiny, fairy-size again.

"It's so good to see you again, Twisty!" Leona declared, giving him a hug. Then she jumped onto his back. They zoomed upwards out of the reach of the smallest goblin, who stood staring sulkily up at them.

"Oh, my ankle hurts!" the goblin on the ground moaned.

Twisty immediately circled in the air and hovered over the goblin. Then a shower of glitter burst from the unicorn's golden horn and encircled the goblin's injured ankle.

"It's all better!" the goblin said in amazement, jumping to his feet. Looking sheepish, he glanced up at Leona and Twisty. "Thanks," he mumbled.

"Come on, let's go," the smallest goblin snapped. "I'm fed up with pesky fairies and silly girls who spoil all our plans!"

"Me too," the other one agreed as they stomped off.

"Girls, you've done it again!" Leona said happily. "Because of you, almost all our Magical Animals are safely back in Fairyland, and can start their training again. We can never thank you enough – but thank you, anyway!"

"Goodbye," the girls called as Leona and Twisty disappeared in a flourish of fairy sparkles.

"It was wonderful to meet a *real* unicorn, wasn't it?" Rachel said, smiling. "Now we only have one day left at camp, and one more Magical Animal to find."

"Yes, Caitlin's ice bear," Kirsty replied. "But that's the problem. The ice bear's special power is courage." She looked solemnly at Rachel. "So, while he's missing, will we be able to find the courage to take on the goblins?"

Leona the Unicorn Fairy has got her Magical Animal back! Now Rachel and Kirsty must help...

# Caitlin the Ice Bear Fairy

"I can't believe it's the last day of our holiday already," Kirsty Tate said sadly, as she finished packing her bag and zipped it shut. She gazed around the cosy wooden cabin where she and her best friend, Rachel Walker, had spent the week with four other girls. They'd been staying at an adventure camp and had taken part in all sorts of activities – exploring caves, canoeing, horseriding – as well as making some very special fairy friends!

The holiday was almost at an end now,

and their room-mates had packed their bags ready to go home. Only Kirsty and Rachel were left in the cabin.

"We've had such brilliant adventures this week," Rachel said, smiling as she thought about them.

Kirsty put on her coat. "Well, the holiday isn't over just yet," she reminded Rachel.

"We've got High Hill to climb in a few minutes...and we've got to find the last Magical Animal, too."

Rachel nodded, an anxious expression appearing on her face. "Oh, I hope we do spot the little ice bear," she said. "I hate thinking of her being lost and alone."

"Or caught by Jack Frost's goblins," Kirsty added. "We can't let that happen."

It was rather cold outdoors, so Rachel

grabbed their hats and scarves. "Come on," she said. "The sooner we get out there and start looking, the better!"

Unknown to everyone else at the holiday camp, Kirsty and Rachel had been having some extra-special adventures...helping the Magical Animal Fairies find their missing animals! Nasty Jack Frost had stolen them, but the clever animals had found a way to escape from his Ice Castle into the human world, where they'd been ever since. So far, the two girls had helped the fairies track down a baby dragon, a magic black cat, a young firebird, a seahorse, a snow swan and a unicorn. But there was still the ice-bear cub left to find.

Rachel and Kirsty went to meet the other campers, who were gathered outside the camp clubhouse. When everyone was there, one of the counsellors, a tall man called Michael, spoke. "It's the camp tradition to climb High Hill together on the last day of our holiday," he said. "And when we get back, we're having a special goodbye party. So if everyone's ready for the hike, let's go!"

Read the rest of

**Caitlin**

**the Ice Bear Fairy**

to find out what magic happens next...